Happy Day
to
Martha
from
Mary 1981

My great-great-aunts, Madalene and Louisa Pasley, were born in 1848
and 1847 respectively – the youngest children in a large Victorian family.
Their father, Admiral Sir Thomas Pasley, Bart., K.C.B., had been
Flag-Captain to the Admiral of the Fleet in the Crimean War, and,
during the years covered by the album, was Admiral Superintendent of
Devonport Dockyard and then Commander-in-Chief at Portsmouth.
The pictures in the album were drawn by the girls between the ages
of 12 and 16. I do not know why they chose to draw themselves rather like
middle-aged spinsters, but presumably it was a private joke.
Whatever their reasons, I think it adds a delightful touch of
eccentricity to the humour of their most original album.

———————————————————————

Tim Jeal

THE ADVENTURES

OF
MADALENE
AND
LOUISA

by L. and M. S. Pasley

Random House   New York

When we were young my sister Madalene and I preferred chasing beetles and butterflies to lessons in the schoolroom.

We explained to a series of daily governesses that we would rather study ENTOMOLOGY than ARITHMETIC – but none of them was interested in beetles and all of them persisted in setting us SUMS.

We escaped by getting up early and setting off on expeditions before their arrival, or staying up half the night to watch a chrysalis change.

The governesses were annoyed when we fell asleep over our lessons. They complained to Papa of our idle disposition and subsequently

left.

 did not like being bothered by governesses He was Admiral Superintendent of Devonport Dockyard and he had many important things to think about.

Here he is with his tall Flag Lieutenant striding round the dockyard discussing repairs to ships of the line,

. . . and making arrangements for DINNER PARTIES

and croquet matches.

As long as he put off finding new governesses we were able to go on entomologising and even make DARING NIGHT EXPEDITIONS.

One day he remembered we were on our own and asked our elder sister Georgie to keep an eye on us. Madalene and I did not get on with Georgie. She had been sent away to a school where she was made to drink quantities of calomel which had made her SOUR.

She thought we were spoilt having lessons at home. Worst of all she disapproved of entomology, especially at night and whenever she came out with us it was bound to RAIN.

On Meadfoot Sands
we left her  sitting
under her umbrella
and found staggering
specimens of seaweed.

Madalene caught a
GIANT CRAB —
or would have
done if Georgie
had not willed it
to find a hole in
the net.

On our next expedition we took the fishing rods Papa had given us, but Georgie did not approve of that either and refused to join us.

She INFURIATED us by taking 'Mr. Rowley' her pet goldfinch with her on expeditions and, when we were not looking, offering him the beetles we had caught.

Madalene decided to get even with Georgie and let out Papa's fierce PARROT

who terrified 'Mr. Rowley' out of his wits.

After that Georgie refused to have anything to do with us and we were on our own again, except once when Papa asked Stevens, one of the dockyard men, to accompany us. But Stevens was even LESS ENTHUSIASTIC about entomology than Georgie or Madalene's dog Jo, who always imagined our latest finds were teasing him.

Jo found beetles as bothering as bathnight, and though Madalene was always thinking up ways of distracting him,

they seldom succeeded.

apa was still too busy to find a new governess, but one day he did take us on his yacht the *FIRE QUEENE*.

He took Georgie too and perhaps that was why it was stormy Georgie went below looking sourer than ever, and we played our violins to prevent ourselves thinking of sea sickness but were soon overcome and had to be put off at Dartmouth

In 1862 we left Devonport for the Lake District.

DEPARTURE OF SIR T.S. PASLEY, AND FAMILY, FROM DEVONPORT TO WINDERMERE.

(Note:— Sir T.S.P. has walked on to the station.)

1. Traction Engine,—commonly called the Elephant.
2. Jo, under the impression he is going to be washed.
3. A few dockyard men come to offer their assistance.
4. Stevens.
5. The Omnibus.
6. Madalene S. Pasley,—packed.

Delighted to be back at **The Craig**, our home near Lake Windermere for the Summer, and fortunately still without a governess, we entomologised night and day while Georgie fussed about indoors.

 he flowers we found

near 'the Craig' were more exciting than

any we had seen at Devonport,

and in the light of the lantern, quite ordinary moths
and beetles looked LARGER and more interesting.

We determined to make the most of our freedom.
One day we harnessed 'Blunderbuss' and set out
in search of ADVENTURE.

Madalene noticed some huge glow worms flying
past and decided to catch one.

She used her whip to secure their leader

but he tried to escape with the assistance of one of his relations

and d-r-a-g-g-e-d his feet to show his indignation.

Meanwhile I encountered a great green grasshopper

and YELLED for Madalene and caught him by the leg.

but the great green grasshopper sprang into the Phaeton
and drove off without us.

That summer we had many other strange adventures
some of which are recorded here :—

The Oil Beetle

1. *We encounter an Oil Beetle.*

2. *'It possesses the property of exuding an unpleasant smelling oil when surprised or touched:— hence its name'.*

3. *Eventually all the oil sank into the ground and the captors returned home in triumph.*

The Dragonfly

1. The Dragonfly resists all attempts at capture

2. Jo joins the fray and grabs him by the leg

3. Whereupon the Dragonfly sheds all his legs

4. enabling us to tie him up

5. and pull him through a stile

6. and finally push him in through the window

THE UNKNOWN LARVA

1. Grand discovery of a
   hitherto unknown larva

2. We remove his dinner

3. His flight

4. We stop him

5. A solid body

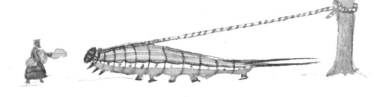

6. Solution of the difficulty

7. In captivity

8. The ferocious animal escapes

9. Tableau

The Privet Hawk Caterpillar

1. We find a Privet Hawk caterpillar in a tree and dislodge it

2. It almost escapes

but agrees to a lift

3. during which a transformation occurs

4. finale

At the end of the summer Papa told us that since
he had been unable to find a suitable governess he
had engaged a drawing master called Mr. PHILIP
MITCHELL. To our dismay Georgie was to have
drawing lessons with us.

Georgie admired Mr. Mitchell and wanted to please him. She told us we were not to tease him just because he felt the cold and went sketching with a cape and a rug. Needless to say Mr. Mitchell had no interest in entomology and wanted us to draw Lake Windermere.

It was not difficult to creep away from Mr. Mitchell leaving him alone.

Occasionally Mr. Mitchell would come and catch us both

or one of us,

and then the other.

But often he gave up in despair, and
we could seek further adventures.

The Rare Larva

We discover a beetle
larva in a dead tree.

With great effort
it is secured

in a collecting case.

It however bursts
the ends out

and another method has to be adopted.

Mr. Mitchell enthused over Lake Windermere and asked us to row him out to see the sunset. He wore his top hat and recited a poem which Georgie thought ROMANTIC.

The trip was such a success that we took him out again—without the boatman with us, we soon found interesting company.

But Mr. Mitchell appeared not to notice anything unusual, even when Jo fellin and Georgie complained about the beetle we had asked her to hold.

Madalene thought how amusing it would be if Mr. Mitchell were to join in some of our adventures, and she drew what might happen to him if he did:—

1. Mr. Mitchell begins to sketch on (as he thinks) a log of wood.

2. It proves to be a 'looper' caterpillar and towards evening it rises erect to sleep.

3. L. & M.P. procure a ladder.

4. The caterpillar feeling tickled doubles half up.

5. Further endeavours at rescue.

6. By a sudden jerk the caterpillar throws Mr. M. to the ground.

7. He is carried home by his pupils on the ladder.

But when Mr. Mitchell saw Madalene's drawings he was so angry his whiskers went stiff with rage. He said we would *never* learn to draw Lake Windermere or anything serious for that matter, and much to Georgie's regret he gave in his notice.

After that Papa decided that we were too old for governesses and too idle for drawing masters so we were able to entomologise as much as we liked with no one to bother us.

We caught a great number of rarities for our collection,

and spent hours studying the habits of
sportive ichneumon flies . . .

until we left Windermere for Portsmouth where Papa had a grand new appointment.

THEN Papa said I could help him arrange parties and croquet matches, which I did (though it always seemed to rain),

Plate I

1. Brimstone Butterfly. 2. female. 3. the caterpillar. 4. chrysalis.

A SELECTION

OF

BRITISH BUTTERFLIES,
& MOTHS.

By MADALENE S. PASLEY.

Authoress of

"Notes on Lepidoptera," &c. &c.

In 2 Parts. PART ONE
Butterflies.

1864.

and Madalene could write books about butterflies and
beetles with proper illustrations, which she did —
but nobody liked them as much as THE ALBUM.

POSTSCRIPT

Madalene married Sir Henry Jenkins, who was
Parliamentary Counsel to the Treasury from 1886-1889.
She founded and for many years edited the
'Mothers Union Journal' – a quarterly with a
circulation of over 200,000 copies.
Madalene died in 1939. Louisa never married
and died in 1929. Both sisters remained
keen entomologists and artists all their lives.
The Craig, where their 'adventures' took place,
was demolished in 1968, An estate of modern bungalows
was built in its grounds.